WHAT IF...

WHAT HAPPENS WHEN THE WHAT-IF'S DON'T SEEM TO GO AWAY

M. AABIDHA THASLIM

Made with ♥ on the Notion Press Platform
www.notionpress.com

Dedicating to

My Mother

Contents

Acknowledgements

My first debt is to the Lord Almighty for his blessings in abundance He showered upon me. I would like to thank my Friend T. Kodeeswari for guiding me to contribute my works of imagination and experience in the field of literature. I thank my Husband Mr. Syed Aziz who appreciated my short stories and also for the cover picture he edited for my book. I extend my gratitude to my family members especially my sister M. Shaamila Thasnim who helped me correcting the script and proof reading the work.

1
THE COTTON

Raghuram was about to leave the house that evening to meet his friends at the place where they used to sit together. Hailing from a traditionally grounded background, everything pertaining to progressive thinking had turned into a taboo for him. His wife was very devoted to Lord Krishna and spent most of her time in the pooja room, reading stories of Mahabharatha. She was a typical traditional woman one could find in a conservative family. She loved her son Santhosh very much. Devaki's decision to spend time in poojas and chanting verses of God itself was a get away from the spiting words of regressive thinking of her husband. As a matter of fact, she disguised herself as overtly religious and secluded herself in the room of deities, incense sticks, and dhoop. Along with the tradition, the regressive ideas about women and their structured lifestyle continued for years in the mind of Raghuram. Devaki, her mother-in-law, and her nieces were not allowed to cook during menstruation. Raghuram was so engulfed in his so-called 'culture' or principles that he restrained himself from looking at the countenance of women during menstruation. Raghuram's son Santhosh secured good ranks in his higher studies and spent his life as a well-reputed engineer in the field of information technology in Chennai. After a few years, he decided to hold hands with Abitha, who was working with him till that date. Abitha's household echoed progressive thoughts in places adjacent to her house. She never believed in superstitions and was always against those culturally regressive thoughts, rituals, and rites. Santhosh's decision to marry Abitha created havoc among the members of his family. Devaki, somehow tried her level best to marry her son off to the girl he loved most, and it was granted on one fine day.

Abitha stepped into the threshold of Raghuram's house and felt strange rituals and rites being conducted every time. Even though she hesitated to stay at that weird mansion for a while, she made up her mind to put up with the inmates of the house for Santhosh.

With his umbrella, Raghuram was about to leave the house when something intrigued his mind in the corner of the house. There was a huge swing in the corner hung from above, swaying between the two pillars. Near the swing, there was a small scaffold, and there was a sanitary napkin pack on it. Abitha had just left the place for an important call and had kept the napkin packet on the scaffold. Raghuram noticed the sanitary napkin packet and shouted at his wife, who had no idea about what had happened in that house. She just turned around from the pooja room and asked what had made him so furious that he shouted like a thunderbolt. Raghuram said, "What the hell did I just see? Who kept this abominable thing here? Can't you hide this object of impurities from my view?" Abitha did not see it coming and stood shocked at Raghuram's remarks about the sanitary pad. Abitha replied, "What's wrong with that? It is just cotton! See?" She took one pad, removed the cover, took the cotton from the pad, and showed him. Her act infuriated Raghuram, and since he could not yell at the new bride, he threw his umbrella in the corner and left the place. At eight at night, Raghuram's entry was unusual. He entered the house completely drenched and humiliated his daughter-in-law with his stare. He had immersed his body into the holy pond in the vicinity and returned home. Abitha found herself in a deep pit of horror. She detested staying at that house and decided to leave the place as early as possible. One Friday, Raghuram and his wife took Abitha to the native temple. She was asked to sit in the back seat, and the stare of accusation still persisted in Raghuram's eyes. On the way, in a car, the small tree in the corner fell on the road by the time the car came near it. Raghuram did not expect the sudden fall of the tree, and it made him go berserk and drove the car to the side where there was a pit. He could not control the steering, and the sudden anxiety made him push the clutch for long instead of brake, and the car hit the other tree. Devaki and Abitha tumbled and jumped from their seats, yet they escaped with minor injuries, or one could say no injuries to mention. Raghuram's head hit the corner of the car glass, and the blood oozed out continuously. No one was there in the middle of the road, and he was almost in a state of unconsciousness. Abitha comprehended the scene, took Raghuram away from the driver's seat, and made him lay under the tree. Devaki could not help him but bawled her eyes out. Abitha opened the bag she had brought with her, took a few things away, tore a few things apart that included her end of the pallu, tied his head tightly to cease the flow of blood. She eventually made a call to an ambulance on time, and Raghuram was sent to the hospital. While he was slowly gaining his consciousness, the medico of that clinic inquired about the incident and appreciated Abitha for her valour. The nurse asked Abitha if she had had a first aid kit inside the car, to which the answer was no. The nurse, puzzled at the materials on the plate which Abitha used to tie Raghuram's head, asked, "Then these?" pointing at them. "This cotton piece?" asked the nurse. "Ha ha, this one? I took it from the sanitary pad I had kept inside the bag. I always carry a pad or two everywhere."

"It is just a piece of cotton, right?" On listening to the conversation, Raghuram's mind returned to its complete state of consciousness, the realization of his perspective. The stare lost its way from his eyes forever.

2

FUNERAL SERVICE LIVE

Kishore, his mother, and his grandfather shifted to the new place after the demise of Kishore's father. Kishore was 9 years old, and he was the apple of his father's eye. His father, Sebastian, and mother, Natasha, met with a fatal accident lately, which cost Sebastian's life, and left Natasha with a fracture in her hand, and a deep wound on her forehead. Sebastian's cousins stayed abroad and were unable to attend his funeral. So, a videographer was arranged for the funeral. The bishops were singing songs of sorrow and prayer songs in front of the mortal remains of Sebastian. One of the bishops read verses from the Bible and associated every human with the verses they read. They sang, "Maranam varum varai," the Malayalam song, usually sung in every Christian funeral. The ceremony was recorded and uploaded on YouTube. Kishore was watching the video of his father while his mother was arranging things in her new house. Natasha grabbed the phone and kept it aside. The song "Maranam varum varai yaavin" echoed in Natasha's ears even though she tried to divert herself from the terrible incident. She was afraid that her son would be deeply wounded by the demise and might not be able to recover from the sorrow. Natasha's father, who was once in the army, consoled her, "Time will heal him, my dear," patting her shoulders slowly.

That night, Natasha tried to sleep peacefully after a long day of work in her new apartment, but the funeral service reappeared in her dream with the countenances of bishops and crying faces. The dream tormented her to the extent that she woke up perspiring and found her son sitting and staring at the dim blue bulb in the room. "Kishore, Kishore," she shook his shoulder. He turned and said, "Amma." "What are you doing? Sleep," she told him, covering his eyes with her hand, and after some time, she tried to pull the blanket close to Kishore.

The next day, Natasha was walking in the market, staring at the prodigious buildings to her side. She did not pay heed to the passersby and accidentally hit a man in his fifties. She turned and said, "Sorry." The grave old man with a long face, holding the Bible, turned at her, stared, and went away. That night, the same song echoed with the funeral service, with the distorted face of a corpse and white flowers arranged everywhere. The bishops sang, as did the singers, "Maranam varumvarai yaavin." Again, she woke up and checked on her son. He was deeply asleep.

The next day, Natasha walked into the same market and found a poster of the deceased. He was none other than the man she had hit the previous day. Shocked by the news, she headed back home and searched for water in the fridge. She was panting while holding the water bottle and gulped the water in a snap of a second. She wanted to inform her father but felt that such an incident could be a coincidence. She decided to take her son, Kishore, to a park adjacent to her house. In the corner of the street was Sundaram Park. Natasha was holding Kishore, directing him to the swing. Suddenly, a ball fell near her. Natasha picked it up and gave it to a young girl and her mom who were approaching her. Natasha returned the ball with a smile. That night, she felt peaceful and retired to bed. Again, she had the same dream, and the same song appeared with the mortal remains, whose faces looked distorted. Natasha felt that the recent incident had hurt her so much. The song of faith and death in Malayalam was sung again. Natasha didn't mind it much since she had lost her husband lately.

The next day, the song echoed in the hall from the

phone. Natasha got annoyed and decided to remove her husband's funeral live service from YouTube. She went to her son to scold him for playing the video of a funeral, thinking that it was that of Sebastian's. But the phone was on the table near the verandah. She took the phone and looked up. The song still played, "Maranan varumvarai yaavin." To her shock, it was not the funeral service of Sebastian because there were two coffins placed there, the coffins of a daughter and her mother whom Natasha had met in the park lately.

3
THE FRAGRANCE

Malini, the name echoed in every hotel and wedding hall. She, being adept at choosing the right flowers for decoration pulled off in the field of horticulture. Her son,

Manoj helped her in flower exports as well. Each and every flower that Malini touched matters the most. She had the knack of converting the least beautiful flower adorned so well in a line. Her workshops were much acclaimed by the students of colleges, entrepreneurs and women at home as well.

The fragrance she had in her personality was adorable. Every flower she touched was believed to be as 'the touch of Midas'. Her "Malini blooms" spread its fragrance everywhere in the events. Fifteen years ago, the half-demolished panchayat school ran in a village where the importance of education was just sprouted. The bathrooms were open at the top and had a huge wall and a gate. Dhanampillai was a big shot in that village of poverty and casteism. The stench from the toilets can be felt during intervals. Only two people were assigned for manual scavenging, that too was on the basis of caste. Young Manoj was heading back to his home with his small bag containing tiny notebooks, passing Dhanampillai's house.

Reclining on the chair Dhanampillai was reading the newspaper. Dhanampillai's wife mumbled over the stench of fecal matter in front of the house. Her youngest son defecated in the morning and left the place. With the sudden drizzle of rain in the morning, the stench spread horribly, and people clipped their nose with their fingers while entering the house. Dhanampillai, observing the boy passing by, called him and asked him to remove the wet stool of human excretion. Appalled by the order, young Manoj hesitated for a while and stood confounded. "Take this paper and remove the poop from the place.

What are you staring at eh? Your mother does this every day right?" Young Manoj felt helpless, his eyes welled up, with his hands he took the wet, abominable excrement, he felt nauseated but couldn't express his agony.

To his age, it was a horrible experience. While taking the filth in his hands, his mother caught him and grabbed the paper from him. She swiftly took the broom from the corner, cleaned the place and took his son back home. She beat him twice and sat in the corner of the hut and cried like a defeated warrior. Young Manoj went back to his mother and said, "Amma, I won't do it again, Ayya only asked me to do it, I don't want you to clean bathrooms amma." She grabbed his hands and said "Your mother's fate is written as such my boy" " I can't get over this pre-written curse. I don't want you to be like me. That's why I send you to school." Both Manoj and his mother were exhausted from crying all day long and dozed off without a meal. The next day Manoj's younger sister was playing in front of her hut. Her mother returned home with a plastic cover containing Jasmine flowers well tied in a string.

She called Mullai and adorned her braided hair with the flowers, said, " I chose the best of flowers, fresh and new and just plucked them in the evening for you, my mother taught me to choose the best of them." "My life was destined to work among the stench, but I want both of you live like blossoms". Her words hit Manoj who was reading the lesson books, so hard and deep and he resolved to get away from his status. He wanted to find a machine to knock out manual scavenging completely but his score in biology was more than the scores he received in physics and social science. His preference bloomed in horticulture and immersed himself more into that field. "Don't add carnation with the roses as they look similar in appearance. Cut the stem carefully, insert the small ones at the bottom of the foam like a Ravenna, place carnation with limited no of leaves." While Ms. Malini was instructing the interns about flower arrangements. Her clients waited for her appointment outside with orders of dahlia, chrysanthemums, roses, lilies and carnations. Meanwhile, Malini dropped a line in her cell phone, "Mullai, your Jasmine flowers are ready, don't forget to wear them for the event".

4

UNSAFE

It had been three days I came to the new building as a tenant. A translator in profession I was a freelance writer and teacher at a school in the vicinity. Being single., I had a few cartons to bring home and unbox them. The house was neither big nor small and loved the terrace with multiple views around which might kindle my mind to write stories and paint pictures. At half past eight in the morning I saw different kinds of responsibilities on the street. Some picked their children for schools. Some waved their baskets with vegetables and green leaves with bent stems at its end. Some carry water pots. I observed everything with a mug of coffee in the terrace. Suddenly I caught a glimpse of a woman, probably twenty or thirty years old carrying a school bag and a lunch bag. Her gait was slightly different from the others I perceived so far. She walked as if somebody was treading by her side. She walked alone and through her props one can assume that she was heading to school. She looked like a typical mother of a five to eight year old. It distracted me yet I went back to my house to get ready for school. Having finished my work in the afternoon I visited my friend and had a good time with him. I admired his paintings which he did as a pro and ordered one for my house as a mark of encouragement.

After a sumptuous lunch I started to my house with the food packet for dinner. I reached home by 3.30 PM and slept. An hour sleep took away my tiredness. I started looking for a location to hang the picture I ordered. I, in a pure white vest and gray pants stared at the wall near the window and asked myself whether the place I fixed for the painting add beauty to the entire room. As I was staring at the wall with hands on my hip, I got distracted by the appearance approaching the window from the other side and who took a turn to the right to enter the threshold of the house opposite to mine. The same woman holding the schoolbag and a lunch bag. The lunch bag was partially heavy and was pink in colour indicating the stereotype that the owner of the bag could be a girl.

At 7. 40 PM while I was checking the texts in my mobile, I heard the sound of a plastic ball bouncing near the house opposite to mine. I found none around but the ball. The woman I saw that day rushed outside and picked the big ball and shut the door. With no conscience I went outside and tried looking through the window of the house. if I could see any child inside. The half-opened screen of the window was pulled by the inmate of the house shutting my view. I learnt from my neighbour that the family residing in front of my house consists of three members; a man and his wife and a child. The man was working as a scientist in Bangalore and he visited once in a fortnight.

Next Day I saw the same woman carrying the bags with slightly different gait. A week passed yet I could not find a child anywhere near the house, nor on the street. One fine evening I was carrying the painting to my house and found the same woman towards me. As I crossed her, I found her murmuring a little as if she was talking to someone beside her. On seeing me she became silent and walked faster than usual. That night I felt that it was unnecessary noticing her and decided not to think about that woman anymore she might be partially disturbed or depressed in mind.

I thought of skipping the whole concept of the woman and her bags. That night I did not feel sleepy and went to the terrace with my phone. There was silence everywhere but with few bulbs lit at some houses. In that grave silence I heard the ball bouncing on the floor and that time the woman did not come running instead I heard the steps of a small child. I rushed to my gate to see who the child was. On seeing the ball hanging in the air, my face turned pale, panic-stricken and found myself at dawn passed out near the front gate. It happened more than two times and I resolved to ask about that to the woman staying in that house. "Sister!" I called her on the road while she was busy buying vegetables on the pavement. I told everything I observed and asked what that apparition was. Her face turned dark and gloomy and rushed back to her house.

I tried sending my neighbour aka friend to her house and gave a couple of visiting cards of the Exorcist and the Psychiatrist. My neighbour was a kind woman of 45 and I found my mother in her and she was adept at convincing others as well. So, I was confident that I might have been of great help to the woman with a "so called" child. Days went by and my neighbour aunt tried many times and decided to act as if she was a skeptic of the woman with madness and it would make her vacate the place. Finally, the woman accepted to reveal my neighbour aunt of the truth that she had two girl children and she lost her eldest daughter in child rape by some men. The other child was her only hope. As the second child was disturbed by the loss of her sister, it would take time for her to be back to her normal self.

Her husband, being a scientist in chemistry resolved to find the product to protect the second child. He invented a cream which makes the humans invisible for a while. The cream would last for half the hour. I felt bad for my deed of interrupting her life yet I learnt how unsafe the girl children were. Felt ashamed of being a part of the society where child abuse and rape became common... Nobody on the street knew the presence of the child. The very night I heard the sound of the ball with no agitation. I sought apology from my God and prayed for the safety of female children. . . Burdened with tears I reclined on the sofa and fell asleep.

5

DEEP SIGH

Ravindher had a massive heart attack in the morning. A seventy-five-year-old widower, a landowner with an ambassador car as his favourite. He roared with his car in his youth and was raised to fame for his majestic looks and financial background, very much grounded to his cultural ethics. He had a daughter, who, at present, was a fifty-year-old mother of two, wife of a businessman. Luxury is the lifestyle bestowed by her husband for her submissive attitude. Her life circled around temples, household chores and children, who had flown to other countries for higher studies. Geetha had been to the temple that day when her father had the attack. He was taken by the servants to the hospital. His grandchildren who came on a vacation fled to the hospital. He underwent Angio surgery quite common among the people in late 50s and above. The surgery was done. The grandchildren in their late twenties took immense care of him. Yet he couldn't come back to his consciousness. Ravinder was in a state of coma which medicos predicted could be short-lived. It all happened before the arrival of his 50-year-old daughter. By the time she arrived at the hospital, it was night and her children headed back home. Only She and her father were there in the luxurious room of the hospital. There was little agitation in the countenance of Geetha. Nothing surprised her nor did she have a shock. She checked his face and sat in the corner. Ravinder had already recovered from the coma and he was asked to take rest which Geetha didn't learn from the doctors.

All she knew was her father was unconscious. She sat on the chair near his bed. " hmm ... sleeping, coma, a kind of hibernation. Something... I really wanted in my life... to sleep, forgetting household chores, children, husband, temple.... and..." sighed, "God "... "but... as usual I was unlucky" unlucky as usual... Ravinder couldn't take rest and he had just closed his eyes, giving rest to his eyes but his ears were conscious and sound as his body and soul. He was listening to his daughter speaking to him. " Lucky man you are! You threatened everyone during your middle age days and you threatened death as well. God has made you strong... strong for your reason. The reason that you wanted and still want others' lives and wishes revolve around you"." So stubborn that you killed; killed the idea of death. With a faint smile of sarcasm, like you killed my soul...my kids from forcible marriage have all grown up now. Hmm, you killed my dreams, my wishes, my likes and dislikes. You never made me live my life... just for loving the guy who couldn't fit into your standards and background, you pushed me to the darkroom, with someone unknown, your son in law. Everything was just forced. Him, children, all against my will. Pushed into prostitution. Not right for a woman like me to use such terms right? still I convince my mind to like, to love him... but failed. Disputes bombarded every time but all I could do was to curl up to the corner and a school dropout, helpless woman, relying completely on the man who I could neither love nor hate. Hmmm. Years passed faster than one's imagination. And I still am passing every day, for hibernation. prolonged ......father, you and your stubborn attitude, your prestige won at last. I failed. " She said, staring at the wall unnoticing him and his small teardrops across his eyes. She moved back home again with a deep sigh. The next day the house where Geetha resided was overcrowded, with garlands and wreathes, friends and family members gathered there. Her father was, still at the hospital, was about to be discharged in two days.... someone in the family who strove and waited long for hibernation had just passed...

6
THE NOTEBOOK

Robin couldn't find any way worthy enough to pull off in his life. Everything he felt went wasted; be it a business or a job. Everything depressed him to the extreme of himself committing suicide. He made up his mind and decided to fall into the nearby well which was abandoned for ages. He gulped the remnant whisky on the table, headed to the abandoned well. The dry leaves made a rustle as he stepped on the dry leaves, crushing them with his dirt blotted shoes. With the pain he couldn't see the small rock ahead, hit his leg and fell, facing the ground. A small leather notebook was lying there. He picked it up slowly, opened it, on the first page, was written ' write on me' in an unknown language. He couldn't understand the inscription, stared confounded, a voice whispered in his ears, "Write on me". It whispered, reiterated many times till he made up his mind to write something. The stylus was attached inside the leather notebook. He took it back home and turned the pages. He read the few lines already written by someone in the first few pages. He just wanted to write as per the order of the whisper. The previous line was, I want to be a millionaire !" He read the line and repeated the same. He wrote with his slightly slanted handwriting, " I want to be a millionaire", period.

The phone vibrated, buzzed for long. He inserted his hands into his pants pocket and took his phone and attended the call. The call was from Juno, his friend. " Robin! Robin! We got a huge order today. They bought all our stuff and credited us with a huge sum. It all happened out of the blue. Robin! Can you hear me! Hello! Hello!" Before Robin could answer the phone hanged up. Robin's eyes filled up, he couldn't believe his eyes he cried in happiness, perspired, shocked in a surprise. He wrote the same line again. " I want to be a millionaire", period. The phone buzzed again. This time was from his uncle who was a real estate owner. " Hello, Rob, Good news for you, the old house you had in the town was sold, do you know how much I sold? 50 million dollars! That old creepy house cost a huge price all of a sudden. There would be a multiplex in that place. Robina, we won man! hello, hello... " beeped. Robin's exhilaration hit the zenith.

He took a deep breath, exhaled, and held his hair with his hands. He couldn't believe his eyes. He was ravenous. The whiskey turned to vapour in his stomach and turned empty. He wrote, "I want sumptuous food". The bell rang in the next second the food delivery boy stood grinning like a happy corpse. " Your friend ordered a treat for you sir" he paid it already. Surprised Robin grabbed the pizza food package, hot noodles, coke, ate them like a starving dog; ate them to his belly stifle. He then went back to the notebook. The small notebook had fewer pages and was already scribbled, he turned them to find a blank, didn't notice that it was another section titled reverse. He turned to the page with half the space on the page.

He, with food in his mind mistakenly wrote "food". All of a sudden, he suffered severe pain. His stomach had convulsions like a cyclone, which coerced him to the toilet. All he had taken went in a flush. He came back gulped a bottle of water from the fridge. Now he found a little space in the notebook. Took the stylus, wrote "I want my family happy." He got a call from his mother wailing deep " Robina, Robina, our girl left us forever aaaa ! She left us aaah..... post...post... Mort..em.. ", the voice stopped. Robin bit his nails, he couldn't believe his fortune, himself, confounded, cried. Yet, he couldn't believe it. He tried calling his mother again. The call was stopped, then again, no signal. Panic stroke him deep on his countenance. He turned the pages. Now, there was little space, he was on the last page of the notebook, the section titled, "the end". The last page had more pathetic scribbles like save me, kill me save me and so many. All such words and phrases echoed in his ears like an abhorrent chant. His one hand and his leg were not in a control. He got the last call, Robin realized that there was no such icon for hang up. He attended the call. it was a chant from an unknown language; whispered by many. He couldn't stop the chant. He threw the phone away, taking a deep breath, he tried writing, " save me" which turned into " kill me" ...he tore it and threw the notebook away. His one leg and his hand didn't work, dragged himself to the wall. His hand throttled him deeply, he scoffed, stifled and hit the nearby table, fell unconscious. The glass vase dangled and hit hard on his neck. The next day, his house was crowded with people around gossiping about the cause of his death. Near the well, the leaves moved in a wind, and there was lying the leather notebook.

7

SHAME

Few more lines appeared with anxiety on the foreheads of Mr.Arun and his wife . They kept their heads down for long, unable to put up with the consoling words of relatives and neighbours. A few of them in the vicinity tried peeping out their heads with curiosity. A few relatives gently patted the shoulders of Arun," It shouldn't have happened to Anita. She should have been a bit more careful of herself; It seems like everyone stares at her" sighed Mr. Batra. Mr. Arun's head had still not been lifted. Media lights and mikes thronged in number in the morning and were sent out, accepting the invitation of the formal press meeting to be held with Anita. The entire room echoed with mild sobs and sighs. Grim looks, doleful faces hovered around and there was hardly any smile in the countenances except in the wall hangings of Anita . Anita, in the other room locked herself and sat idle on the cot with extreme calmness around. Her eyes were slightly drooped out of weariness and that too she had after cried for a while. Her pet dog tried pretending to be in a pensive mood like his master. He sat next to Anita with the comfort feeling of being with someone he loves the most. That evening the hall was filled with jostling press reporters with their mikes of different sizes and shapes kept together on the table in the front. It was Anita's press meet to share her reaction for her being captured nude at the reputed hotel bathroom where she was asked to stay at night for an interview she had for the next day. The pictures were leaked for the public to view on websites and one black sheep came across the snaps, informed his uncle Mr. Arun about his daughter. The story, eventually appeared on dailies and ravenous Tv channels for TRP.As is the society so are the people and especially relatives made mountains of the issue, worrying about her future and her impending orphaned, unmarried status all her life. She sat in the middle chair with her parents on either side. The reporters and the police hushed each other. One of the reporters slowly posed the usual frivolous question to Anita. "What did you feel when you saw yourself naked in the picture Anita?"

The eyes of the reporters almost protruded to know her answer. Anita slowly replied exhaling her breath as if she had held it for long. "I saw myself; naked with shoulders broader,with birth parts visible, I saw my hand, my arms, my thighs and I realized stretch marks on them. I didn't look lean. it was a celluloid figure I have right now. I think, I should consult a good trainer for workout. " With her reply everyone's mouth stayed wide agape, with an unanticipated look. Her parents looked at her, wondered if she was the same one who cried last night. she stood up, holding her parents and left the place with the shouts of "Madam" instead of "Anita".

8

MIRACLE

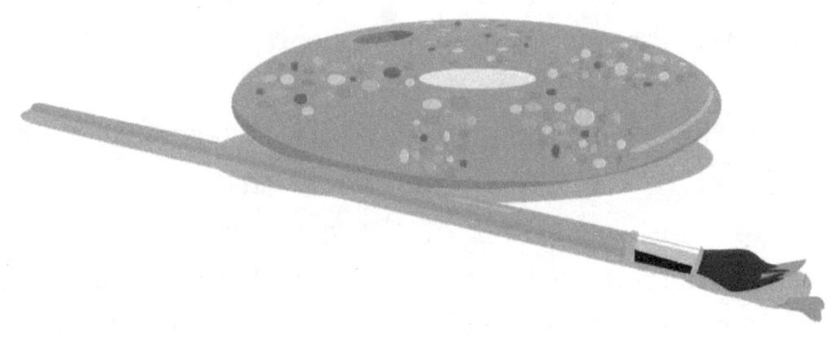

Ankita was in the final year of her undergraduate course and she loved participating and organising events. She had a sister who had joined in the first year of the same major Ankita chose in humanities. Ankita knew very well that her sister was good at pencil sketching and painting. She won a few prizes in her primary school days. After fifth grade, her sister was admitted to another school where competitions held once in a blue moon and that too for those favoured by the teachers. Her sister never got the opportunity to participate yet she continued drawing in her rough notebooks during the time of leisure. Ankita decided that she should help her sister participate in many completions held at the college by many departments on various occasions. Once a painting competition was held by the Library Service Committee. Ankita got wind of the event and rushed to her sister and asked her to enroll her name in that competition.

She went to the library to register her name but it was too late. Only 22 students can participate in it and it was full by the time her sister went there. Ankita felt bad on knowing that and she consoled her sister that she would inform her of some other event as early as possible.

On the day of competition Ankita's sister went to give attendance in the library and learnt that one girl didn't turn up. The authorities of the event asked her if she could participate in the competition. Ankita's sister said "yes" but she had no pencils or colour paints with her. The authorities asked the other competitors to aid her. She got a few items and started working on them. In the meantime, the other girl who had already given her name for the event appeared after a few minutes. The authorities felt that they couldn't ask Ankita's sister Beena to quit. So, they included the other girl and changed the number of participants into twenty-three. With the help of few colours she borrowed from her collegemates, Beena drew the picture. The day of winners' announcement came and Beena was awarded the second prize. Everyone shook hands with her. From then She inserted many certificates into a leaf file. God identified Beena and let the unchangeable terms and conditions of the competition loose. After a decade Ankita and Beena still reminisce that moment and smile.

9
CRAYONS

Still I remember the days when I was in the first standard. My school was adjacent to my house. I lived in a two-storeyed house which only a few had built in the early 90s. I was asked by my drawing miss to bring the crayons pencil box and that was the first time I saw how crayons were. As nagged by me, my father bought a crayons box. It was a cardboard box with the slide. As instructed, I wrote my name with an initial and gave it to my miss. She kept it safe.

While using crayons we had the habit of looking at others' boxes. Some envied, some looked with awe at the boxes with more than 12 colours. The school remained closed owing to unexpected flood which collapsed properties and lives of animals. my father and others swam to get and distributed foods. It lasted for more than a week and we returned to our schools after ten days.

During art and crafts period my miss brought a box with all leftover somewhat good crayon pens. All mixed up and we took some broken crayon pencils of different colours. We took whichever remnant was there and used to colour the picture. The flood washed away the budding emotions within us. Nothing remained in the flood; neither our crayon box nor our identity, so are our pride and envy...

www.ingramcontent.com/pod-product-compliance
Lightning Source LLC
La Vergne TN
LVHW041259150826
845673LV00008B/2662

* 9 7 9 8 8 9 3 2 2 2 4 0 1 *